Free to Learn

(frē)   (lurn)

by Thomas S. Owens

Perfection Learning®

Cover Illustration: Phyllis Pollema-Cahill
Inside Illustration: Phyllis Pollema-Cahill

Dedication
To Reverend Dagoberto Zelaya, Teacher of Freedom

About the Author

Thomas S. Owens is married to Diana Star Helmer, another author of children's books. Thomas is the author of more than 40 books, including *Collecting Basketball Cards* (Millbrook Press). He likes walking with Diana, cooking soups, gardening, watching cartoons, surfing the Internet, playing with Angel the cat, and living in Iowa.

Image credits: Library of Congress pp. 50, 52 (top);
All other images came from Art Today

Printed in the United States of America. For information, contact
Perfection Learning® Corporation, 1000 North Second Avenue,
P.O. Box 500, Logan, Iowa 51546-0500.
Phone: 1-800-831-4190 • Fax: 1-712-644-2392
Paperback ISBN 0-7891-5164-2
Cover Craft® ISBN 0-7807-9314-5
7 8 9 10 11 12 PP 11 10 09 08 07 06

Contents

Chapter 1

Dame School

James, Jacob, and Jane Blackwell watched their mother. She gripped her pointer. It had been carved from a birch tree limb.

Mrs. Blackwell gripped the stick like a sword. She sliced the air with it.

"This will do," she said. "I'm ready. March, children!"

The children knew their mother treated each day like a battle. The rest of the village knew her as

Dame Blackwell. She ran a Dame School.

"This is more than a child learning to read and write," she once told Jane. "This is the first time a child will learn how to be a good citizen."

Jane was 11 years old. She had finished Dame School long ago. Her job now was taking care of her brothers. And she helped at the school.

Mrs. Blackwell had to earn money by teaching. Once she had spent all her time being a mother. That was before her husband died.

A widow is a woman whose husband has died.

Villagers thought Mrs. Blackwell would move away after that. Most **widows** went to live with relatives.

"This is our home!" she told everyone. She made that home into a school.

The big room where the Blackwells cooked and ate became a classroom. ~~benches~~ awaited children each

st and your
~~B~~lackwell said to
She proved her warning on the first day of school.

Mrs. Blackwell asked Jacob to hand out the **hornbooks.** He loved the feel of the wooden handles.

A clear sheet on top of the

the Lord's Prayer were often written on the paper. The paper was covered with a thin see-through sheet. This sheet was made from a bull's or other animal's horn.

hornbook' never heard of it

words made them glow yellow in the morning light. The words almost floated in air.

The golden hornbooks made Jacob think of the church's small window. Church didn't seem so long when the sun danced in on a Sunday morning.

Jacob stopped to remember. Thwack! His bottom stung.

"Master Blackwell, your job is not finished," said his mother. "As your teacher, I will find you a better job."

She yanked him to the front of the room. She plopped Jacob on a stool. She hung a sign around his neck. It said Idle Boy.

"If you speak, you cannot study with us," she warned. "Children, please look at what happens when you do not obey." Her stick pointed at Jacob.

The back door shook from loud knocking. "Eyes front, children!" Mrs. Blackwell demanded.

Jane opened the door. Benjamin Freeman stepped in.

Benjamin farmed on the edge of town. He came to town weekly to sell vegetables from his garden.

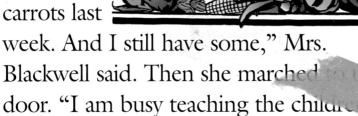

"I bought carrots last week. And I still have some," Mrs. Blackwell said. Then she marched to the door. "I am busy teaching the children."

Benjamin looked left and right. He leaned close and whispered. "I am not here to sell you food," he said. "I do not want your money. I want your teaching."

Chapter 2

The Secret Student

"Close the door, Jane!" Mrs. Blackwell ordered.

Jane Blackwell stood in the doorway. Her eyes were huge. She looked from Benjamin to her mother.

"Dame Mother . . . I mean, Mama . . . uh, Mrs. Blackwell," Jane stuttered.

Mrs. Blackwell grabbed her daughter by both shoulders. She shook her. "Jane!"

Jane looked around the room. "But, Mother!"

Mrs. Blackwell stared at Jane. "You must be the teacher now. I need to speak to Benjamin."

Jane blinked and blinked. Then she took over the class.

Mrs. Blackwell scooted the visitor to the corner of the room. She didn't want the children to hear.

"You?" asked Mrs. Blackwell. "You want to be a student? You are a grown man! A black man."

Benjamin Freeman smiled. "In my heart, I am young. I bought my freedom just this year. For me, my wife, and my three children. As a free man, my life has just begun."

"But why me?" she asked. "I cannot teach you special skills."

Benjamin shook his finger. "A seed cannot become a flower without being planted in the ground. My mind cannot grow until someone plants something in it."

Mrs. Blackwell sighed. "Benjamin, you are a fine farmer. But why do farmers need schooling?"

Benjamin's mouth dropped open. "I want to be more than a fine farmer. I want to be a fine person! A person who can read the Bible. A good father who can read to his children."

Benjamin swept his hand toward the class. "I wish my children could fill your seats," he said. "But I know how the townsfolk are scared of us."

"Change scares them."

Mrs. Blackwell smiled. "You are a very brave man!"

Benjamin looked shocked. He covered his mouth with a huge, dark hand. "Forgive me, Mrs. Blackwell," he said. "I am not brave. I just want a better life for my sons.

"Noah was born two years ago," he continued. "Abraham is three. David is four. They are brave. For they face the future."

Mrs. Blackwell bit her lip. She turned fast. The children who had strained to overhear sat up straight again.

"My students accept you," she said. "But I worry that townsfolk will tease you."

Benjamin nodded. "I know that some townsfolk do not like me. Maybe they don't like anyone who looks like me. That is why I will not tell anyone of your kindness."

Mrs. Blackwell looked at her class again. The students knew Benjamin. They often saw him selling vegetables.

"Benjamin, bring me some of your carrots at this time tomorrow."

Benjamin hung his head. "I understand."

"Do you?" Mrs. Blackwell asked. "You think I want carrots? No. But everyone else will think that.

"You will not be my food **peddler.** You will be my secret student."

A peddler was a person who sold things door-to-door.

Chapter 3

Learning to Learn

Benjamin obeyed. He knocked on the door of Dame Blackwell's school the next day. "Carrots for sale!" he sang.

Mrs. Blackwell rolled her eyes. She showed only a thin smile. "We've been waiting for you," she said.

Benjamin leaped into the room. Jane closed the door quickly.

The other children pushed together on the bench. They looked wide-eyed at the big man and at one another.

"You sit by him," one five-year-old hissed to another. "I don't want him sitting on me!"

Benjamin sat down fast. He folded his hands. Benjamin acted like he was in church.

Jacob smiled at Benjamin. "Here is your hornbook. I can help you."

Benjamin smiled. "God bless you," he whispered.

Mrs. Blackwell clapped her hands. "Children . . . I mean, students!"

Jane giggled.

"Our new student is Benjamin Freeman. Benjamin, we will be talking about our names today. Who can tell me where his or her name came from?"

Jacob's hand shot up. He stood when his mother called on him.

"I have the name of my grandfather. But he died before I could tell him I was using it."

Jane couldn't help giggling again. But she stopped when Mrs. Blackwell glared at her.

"Well, Ben, let's talk of last names. Your last name must be the same as the family that once owned you. Correct?" the teacher asked.

Ben chuckled. "Oh, no, ma'am. My heart named me."

Mrs. Blackwell frowned. Her frown stopped the giggles of the younger students.

"Can you explain?" she asked.

Ben rubbed his hands together. He grinned. "When I bought my freedom, I never thought of names," he said. "People knew my face. They knew me by my hard work. I was just Ben."

"Where did your last name come from then?" asked Ellen White. She leaned forward on the bench to look at Ben.

Ben thumped his chest with his fist. "From me! I got a paper when I first bought my land. It showed it was mine."

"The seller reminded m̶e̶ ̶t̶h̶ free man," he continued. "Then he asked my name. So he could write it on the paper.

"That's when I knew! I knew my name! Freeman!"

Mrs. Blackwell nodded. "Free Man. Or, Freeman."

Ben smiled. "That name is like a song. I love those words!"

Chapter 4

Surprises at School

A week passed. Ben learned more words to love.

First came the alphabet.

Every day, Mrs. Blackwell read from the hornbook. "A. B. C."

The students said the letters back to her.

At day's end, Mrs. Blackwell told the students, "Share your letters at home tonight!" She knew that many students had older brothers and sisters to help them practice.

```
ABCDEFG
HIJKLMN
OPQRST
UVWXYZ
1234567890
abcdefghijklm
nopqrstuvwxyz
```

Ben had no one. There was no one at home to help him read or write. Mrs. Blackwell worried he might learn more slowly than the others.

But every day Ben came. And every day, he said the letters.

Then one day Ben came and sat quietly. He moved his lips fast. But no words came out.

One girl on the bench elbowed a boy beside her. They both stared.

"Ben!" Mrs. Blackwell said. "Stop that. Stand!"

Ben stood. His smile was big as the sun.

"Please speak so we all may hear!"

Ben nodded. "Thank you, Dame Blackwell," he said. "A. B. C. I know. A, B—me!"

21

Mrs. Blackwell shook her head. "Ben, what are you saying?"

Jane clapped her hands. "I know! Ben starts with the letter *B*."

Mrs. Blackwell smiled. "Correct, Ben. But we must finish our practice. Class?"

The students repeated the alphabet.

Next, Mrs. Blackwell read the Lord's Prayer. She read two words. The students said those two words. They pulled their fingers across their hornbooks, pointing at each word.

"Amen," Mrs. Blackwell finished.

"Amen," the children echoed.

"A-ben!" shouted a voice. All the students laughed.

Mrs. Blackwell knew who shouted. "Benjamin! Quiet. Everyone!"

But Ben had been quiet too long. "I know! I know! Mrs. Blackwell, I have learned!"

"What have you learned?" she asked crossly.

Ben pounded his finger on his hornbook. "See? 'Amen.' Ah-meh-nuh. Now, say Ah-Beh-nuh. A. B. E. N!"

"Silence, class!" Mrs. Blackwell shouted. "What you just said is not a word, Benjamin."

But Jane smiled too. She nodded her head. "Go on, Ben."

"Miss Jane knows!" sang Ben. "Throw away that 'ah' letter. I will take the B, E, and N. I heard the word. Now, I see it. My name!"

Mrs. Blackwell nodded. She watched tears fall from Ben's cheeks. He was too happy for any more words.

"Class, Ben has just learned to spell his name. We all can learn our names. Soon. But not today. Class dismissed."

All the students ran outside. Ben walked to the front of the room. He put his hand over his heart. "Thank you. Thank you both."

He waved good-bye and ran outside.

Mrs. Blackwell went to close the door. But a visitor was holding the door's handle.

"Mayor Bennett! Greetings," Mrs. Blackwell said.

"My visit is not a happy one," said the town leader. "I fear you are breaking the law."

Chapter 5

Teaching Troubles

"No! My mother is good!" shouted Jacob Blackwell.

Mrs. Blackwell roughly herded her sons outside. "Mind your tongue!" she hissed. "Be gone, now!"

She slammed the door. "Forgive the children, mayor. They look out for me since their father died."

Mayor Bennett nodded. "I remember. The town leaders did not like a woman living here alone. But you have proven yourself in shaping the minds of our children."

Mrs. Blackwell looked to the dirt floor. She curtsied her thanks.

The mayor stopped. He took a deep breath. "But I fear you wish to trick the town. Townsfolk see that new black man at your school each day."

Mrs. Blackwell tried to pretend. She scratched her head.

"Who?" she asked. "Oh. You mean the food peddler. He is just a farmer. He says his name is Freeman. From the edge of town. Fine carrots. Let me go get some for you to try."

The mayor shouted. "Come back, Mrs. Blackwell."

Mrs. Blackwell stopped. "Yes?"

Tapping his foot, the mayor growled. "There is a law against teaching slaves to read and write. Beware."

She shook her head. "Teaching?"

The mayor stomped his foot. "Do not play games with me! I think you sneak the farmer into school. I think you are teaching him!"

Mrs. Blackwell's smile disappeared. She stared into the mayor's eyes.

"I do not teach the law, sir," she began. "But someone should teach law to you. Benjamin Freeman is a freed slave. He is the property of no one. How will I break that law if I teach him?"

Anger bubbled from the mayor. His voice grew lower but louder.

"I will not see this village host a Negro Dame School. Words have power!" he said. "When you teach Negroes to read and write, you arm them with a powerful weapon."

A weapon, Mrs. Blackwell thought. She saw the pointer on her chair. If a student were as rude as the mayor, she would . . .

Mrs. Blackwell smiled at the idea. Then she quickly turned back to the mayor.

"Anyone who learns has a tool," she said. "Mayor, reading and writing are like a shovel and an ax. They are tools to help a person make more. To do more. To be more."

The mayor threw up his hands. He did not give up, however.

He turned at the door. "I have warned you, Mrs. Blackwell. It would be a shame if you couldn't earn money to care for your children. The village would have to find a good home for them."

The mayor opened the door and stomped away.

Chapter 6

Fearing the Future

The Blackwell children thought they would explode with questions that night. But they knew their manners.

Children were not allowed to speak at the dinner table. But worry made them forget manners. Even the smallest noise would make Mrs. Blackwell jump.

"Does the mayor hate us?" James asked.

"Does everyone hate us?" Jacob asked.

"Can you keep the school open?" Jane asked.

Mrs. Blackwell snorted. "The mayor is angry. He speaks before he thinks."

Jane asked, "Should we leave town? Do we have relatives who will care for us?"

Mrs. Blackwell dropped a wooden plate. "I'll have no more of this talk."

The children looked at one another. And there was no more talk.

At last, Jane cleared the table. Then she added wood to the fireplace.

The boys inched near the light of the fire. They rolled marbles as quietly as they could. They stopped when Mrs. Blackwell appeared with the Bible. She always read verses to the family before bed. But tonight, she didn't.

"We must go to bed early, children," she warned. "Pray that peace returns to the school."

The three young Blackwells obeyed. The next morning, they did everything they always did. They marched when Mrs. Blackwell told them. The boys went to their bench to sit. Jane was ready to pass out the hornbooks.

Except no other children had come to Dame School.

At last, the door opened. It was not Benjamin with his carrots. It was William Morton. He was the only student to come to class.

"Sit!" Mrs. Blackwell ordered. "You are late!"

But William did not sit. He bowed. Then he began speaking.

"I am sorry, Dame Blackwell. My mother wishes me home. And I cannot come back. None of the children can. My mother says you can teach just the farmer. Good-bye."

The door slammed as William ran outside. Jane began to cry. Just then Ben came to the door.

"Carrots!" he called.

"No school today, Ben," Mrs. Blackwell said. "School may be over forever."

Mrs. Blackwell snapped her birch stick in half. The wood dropped to the floor. She walked outside.

"Ben," Jane said. "The town knows you are learning here. Mother was told there will be trouble if you keep coming. The families have kept her students home. Now, no one will pay us. What can we do?"

Ben dropped his carrots. He patted Jane's shoulder. "Do not cry," he begged. "I will not stay to watch this school die. I will do no more learning here. Tell the townsfolk. They can send their children back without fear."

Ben sighed. He started to walk away.

"Wait!" Jane blurted. "Wait. Ben. What if we work together? Perhaps we can teach everyone a lesson."

Chapter 7

Making the Grade

"Mother!" Jacob shouted.

"There she is," James yelled.

They found Mrs. Blackwell sitting on a tree stump. She wiped tears from her eyes. She hugged both boys when they ran to her.

"Ben ran away. He will not come back," Jacob said.

"Jane went to his farm to buy vegetables today," James said. "Ben said you should not be seen with him."

Mrs. Blackwell shook her head. "Seen with him?"

"Yes, those were his words," James said.

Mrs. Blackwell took the boys back to the house. She cooked and cleaned. In the afternoon, she went through the village. She told every family that Benjamin Freeman would not be visiting her school ever again. She told the mayor first.

Mayor Bennett grinned. "You're a wise teacher, Mrs. Blackwell," he said. "I am sure your students will feel better tomorrow."

When Jane came home, she carried a sack. It was stuffed with potatoes and corn.

"We have no money for such food!" Mrs. Blackwell protested.

"Mother, Ben wishes to pay us for your past teaching," Jane said. "I am to visit twice weekly. Ben wishes us to have food payments."

Mrs. Blackwell shook her head. "I should collect them. I feel wrong that he has left."

"No," Jane said. "The townsfolk would grow angry if you visited Ben often. I am only a girl helping her mother get food."

Mrs. Blackwell nodded. Throughout the summer, Jane made trips two times each week. She then returned with loads of food.

Summer ended. On the last day of September, a wagon pulled up in front of the Blackwell Dame School.

Ben was driving. A woman and three boys sat in the wagon.

All the students ran outside. So did Jane and Mrs. Blackwell.

"I had to say good-bye to my two teachers," Ben called.

Mrs. Blackwell turned. She looked at Jane. Jane smiled.

"I taught Ben at his farm," Jane said. "I didn't want you to know. I was afraid you would be in more trouble."

Ben laughed. "Ben couldn't go to the school. So the school came to Ben!"

Mrs. Blackwell looked at the full wagon. "Where are you going?"

"Who knows?" Ben asked. "We sold the crops. We sold the farm. We are teachers now."

Jane smiled bigger. "Ben and his family want to travel. They want to teach other Negroes."

Ben nodded. "If Miss Jane can bring the school to me, we can take the school to anyone."

Mrs. Blackwell went inside. She returned with a gift. She handed Benjamin a hornbook. "Farmers need tools. So do teachers. You are a teacher now."

They waved good-bye. All the children returned to their seats. William Morton raised his hand. "Are you teaching today?" he asked.

"I am learning today," Mrs. Blackwell said.

Chapter 8

Colonial Schools

*I*magine going to your teacher's house. The trip wouldn't be just a friendly visit. You would be going to school there every day.

That's how Dame School worked. It was school at the teacher's house. It was different from schools today.

Parents decided how old their children should be when they started school. There were no laws saying children had to go to school. And the law didn't say how long a school year should be.

Lessons were not fancy. Hornbooks were used to learn reading and writing. Each student had a hornbook. It looked like a paddle with printing on both sides.

A hornbook wasn't a whole book. It was only two pages glued to the paddle.

Horn meant two things. The handle students used to hold the printing looked like a horn.

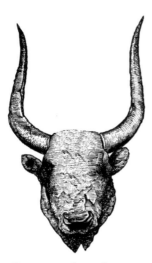

And a thin layer of a cow horn made a see-through covering for each page. The cow-horn sheet protected the paper. Sort of like today's plastic!

Most hornbooks included the Lord's Prayer and the alphabet. Some had word parts such as *-ad, -in, -or,* and *-et.*

The Bible was the easiest book to find in the 1700s. Many parents thought the Bible provided the best education. There were no books written just for young children in colonial times.

What about pencils and paper? Paper was hard to make or find. Thin bark from birch trees was used for paper.

 Children often used chunks of lead or coal to write with.

Students learned reading and writing. That was their only job at Dame School.

What if a student could read and write everything on the hornbook? Then that student was finished. Many students were finished with school for good.

Most girls were kept home. At that time, adults thought girls only needed to know how to cook, sew, and clean.

If parents thought girls needed more education, they taught their daughters at home.

The law said boys should go to school. But some small towns didn't have the money to build schools.

When a town had a school, each family had to pay the male teacher. His job was "schoolmaster." Schoolmasters wouldn't always get money as pay. They would be paid in corn, meat, or whatever families could share.

Learning how to behave was important at school. Students could be whipped with birch limbs. Signs would be hung around students' necks if they were bad.

Boys used *The New England Primer* as their textbook. The book was religious. It had many prayers. But it had rhymes too.

By age 12, many boys were done with school. They could think about college. But most thought about getting jobs.

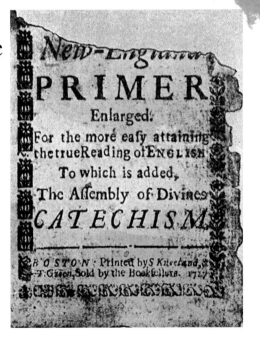

Chapter 9

No Reading, No Writing

Many laws were passed in the 1700s. Some said it was a crime for slaves to read or write. Teaching them was also a crime. A few schools were formed to help black people. The Catechism School for Negroes was founded in New York City in 1704. The school taught a religious education. It helped blacks learn to read the Bible.

However, the school was closed in 1712 because of a revolt. Whites felt that if slaves could read and write, they could send messages. They could tell one another when to meet and when to revolt.

Some slaves had fought their white owners to win freedom. Other whites were killed too. As a result, everyone feared black people who could read or write.

That same fear rose again in Charleston, South Carolina. Slaves started a riot on September 9, 1739. Spanish **missionaries** were blamed. The government said the missionaries encouraged the slaves to fight for their freedom.

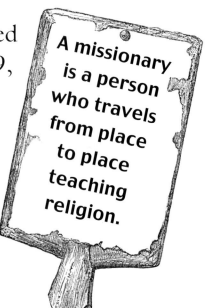

A missionary is a person who travels from place to place teaching religion.

In 1740, the South Carolina Assembly met. The lawmakers banned teaching slaves to read and write.

Hiring blacks as scribes was a crime. That meant even a free black person could not get work reading or writing for others.

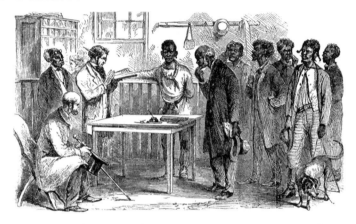

Many whites thought educated freed slaves would use their knowledge to help others escape. They thought reading and writing gave black people power. Maps could be read. Papers showing ownership of property could be written. And papers proving freedom could be understood. White people would not be able to keep as many secrets.

Anthony Benezet started a Quaker School for Blacks in Philadelphia in 1770. For years before slaves were freed, members of the Quaker religion thought slavery was evil.

Quakers invited black children to learn with whites. The school founder said his black students were as good as his white students.

In other words, Quakers thought that all people deserved the chance to learn. Schools could teach more than thinking about words and letters. Schools could teach new ways of thinking about life.